Knight School by Chris Allton

Knight School
Copyright © Chris Allton, 2021
First published by Chris Allton 2021 via Amazon Kindle Direct Publishing
www.chrisallton.co.uk
ISBN – 9798515840549
Front cover design © 2021 by Chris Allton

For Adam (an amazing TA and Ron fan)

"Give me all the bacon and eggs you have."

Chapter 1

"Adam. Adam!!" The master of the house bellowed from his throne for his young slave. "I think I had an accident in my armour, so you may need to wash it out thoroughly." This thought did not fill Adam with much delight. He decided for now not to reply to his master as a date with a smelly piece of armour was not high on his list of priorities today. Adam continued sharpening a sword with a giant stone wheel, rotated by a pedal he pressed up and down under his foot.

Adam was a page to Sir Wilf of Whiffington, the old lord and master of all the land around, and all those who lived upon it. You may be unfamiliar with the term 'page' so let me explain. A page was a servant to a nobleman or knight. This job usually started at the age of seven and involved many tasks including the following:

- Running messages
- Cleaning clothes, armour and weapons
- Learning the basics of combat
- Dressing the master for battle (or indeed any occasion)

This may not sound the most glamourous job in the world but as a seven-year-old child, it was a great privilege to serve the master of the land you live upon and that is because of what you get in return.

Not only is being a page a job, but it is also training. Training to become a squire and then, eventually, to become a knight, just like the master they have served.

So along with all the, unpleasant jobs, come a list of skills the page will learn:

- Horse riding
- Hunting
- Hawking
- Combat
- Playing musical instruments
- Composition and singing of songs

This along with clothing, accommodation, food and learning good manners suitable for that of a knight of the realm. All in all, this seemed quite a fair trade but there could be one big downfall. If the lord the page served was involved in a battle, then the page may well be involved in it also. This was not good.

At the age of fourteen, if the master thinks it is appropriate, the page may become a squire. The tasks were similar, but obviously more skilled and it may involve carrying the master's shield, saddling the horse or holding the lord's flag whilst riding into battle. A squire may also need to guard prisoners or replace an injured horse. Then, finally, by the age of twenty-one, the squire may become a knight and have his own page or squire.

The boy hoped one day to be a knight. Not like Sir Wilf as he was not a good role model. He had seen other knights passing through the lands he lived and gazed in wonder as they rode through, often stopping for a break, to rest their horse or have a tankard of ale with the master.

He loved looking at the shields and crests of the passing knights, comparing one to another and having his favourites. He thought about imaginary battles between various knights, then pitting the winners against the next knight who may arrive in the town.

Being a page was a good thing. Being a page for Sir Wilf was not. He was a very lazy knight and he did not look after his people very well. Adam was nearly ten, having been a page for almost three years. In that time, he had seen other pages not become squires and other squires not become knights.

Sir Wilf was not particularly good at encouraging the best out of his subjects. Not only was he incredibly old but he was very selfish. He just wanted to always keep things the same and have nothing new. This involved the people around Adam. There were other pages around him who should have become squires and knights but Sir Wilf did nothing. In fact, all he did was sit upon his old wooden throne either eating or sleeping most of the day.

Promotion did not look promising for the young page but there was another option and that was Knight School.

Knight School was exactly what it sounded like. A school to learn to be a knight. Everyone who graduated from Knight School went on to become a successful knight so obviously places at this school were high in demand.

So how does a page get into Knight School? Well, the first thing is they have to be recommended by a current knight. As Adam only knew one knight (Sir Wilf) this limited his chances hugely. Sir Wilf would not promote his pages, let alone send them off to Knight School.

Adam had tried many times to interest Sir Wilf in this but with no success. He had tried subtly by bringing Knight School up in conversation, for example

"Did you ever go to Knight School?" he would enquire.

"What?" came Sir Wilf's response.

"Did you ever go to Knight School?" came the repeated question.

"Might school? I might school what?"

"Knight not might!" he replied

"Night night? It's not bedtime, it's still light outside."

"Oh forget it," and off the young page would trudge, downhearted and defeated. This repeated several times but still no joy.

Adam needed another plan. Maybe being a little more direct.

"Ah, boy, you said you had a question for me..." Sir Wilf asked as Adam was clearing away his plates after a meal.

"Yes, I wondered if you could tell me about how a page gets into Knight School." Then came Sir Wilf's reply.

"In my day there was no such thing as Knight School, we became knights by hard work. Look at me. I did lots of hard work." The page found this hard to believe as Sir Wilf never did anything himself. He even needed help going to the toilet and getting in bed. Still no luck so a direct way next.

"Will you put me forward for Knight School?" Adam blurted out one day, directly to Sir Wilf.

"No," came the reply from the grumpy old man. The page sighed. It seemed he would have to take things into his own hands.

Chapter 2

As it turned out, it did not take long for things to change for Adam. One week before his tenth birthday, he received some news that would change his life forever.

"He's only gone and died on the toilet," Eleanor reported trying to hold back a smile. "He had his armour on again and got stuck on the loo. There he fell asleep and passed away peacefully." This was big news for Adam. Eleanor, the girl who had given the news, was his best friend. They had been friends as long as they could remember and had played together as children.

Adam could not remember his parents and could only remember growing up in the house and being a page. Eleanor worked in the house also in the kitchens but like him, she also wanted to go to Knight School.

This was even trickier than it was for Adam as traditionally knights had been male but this was the 1500's so it was about time for a bit of change and females should have equal rights as men. However, this was not the case.

Now Sir Wilf had sadly died, Adam saw this as an opportunity to do something new. He could wait and see who the new Lord of the land would be, but this could take weeks, months or even years to sort out and he was in no mood to wait that long.

"I'm going to travel to the city and join Knight School," he announced the next morning. Eleanor had said her mother would let him stay with them a while, for which Adam was profoundly grateful, but he had made his mind up.

Eleanor realised that once Adam had made his mind up there was no changing it. He told her he was destined to be a knight and she believed in him. She thought that if he put his mind to it then he was capable of anything.

So on the day before his tenth birthday, he packed up his few possessions in an old, hessian, potato sack and set off for the city.

This journey would take a few days and Adam would spend his tenth birthday alone and on the road. He had been walking for a few hours, daydreaming of jousting with other knights and entering a battlefield upon a tall, brightly decorated horse when the behaviour of an old man in the road dragged him back into reality with a shock.

This old man, who reminded him of Sir Wilf in many ways, both in looks and actions, was stood with a long wooden cane in his hand, whipping a horse that had fallen in thick mud. The page could hear the man shouting obscenities at the horse and complaining that he could not get his things to market.

"Don't be so cruel!" Adam protested as he got closer.

"Be quiet boy, this is nothing to do with you," retorted the grumpy old man.

"Stop hitting that horse!" the young boy continued angry at his previous response.

"It's lame, it's no use, it's had it. Time for it to be put down, useless thing." The man walked towards the cart the tired horse was pulling and lifted a blanket, pulling out a sword.

"'Bout time you were put out of your misery," the man bellowed at the horse.

"You will do no such thing," he reacted and jumped in between the old miser and his horse. With this, the old man tried to attack Adam but the boy was having nothing to do with this. He pulled out his trusty wooden sword and waved it at the man. Although a wooden sword was no match for an adult metal sword, he knew right from wrong and felt it important to stand up for the underdog or underhorse in this case.

After a few choice words from the old man he decided that he was going to teach Adam a lesson.

"Young pages like you should be seen and not heard, you will feel the back of my hand." He made tracks to grab Adam but the young boy was having none of it and stood strong, cracking the old man across the knuckles every time he came close.

The poor horse was neighing frantically for not only was it injured but also stuck and sinking in thick black tar like mud. The more he tried to defend the horse, the more he found himself struggling to move in the mud and this caused much hilarity for the old man.

"Look at the pair of you, stuck there. What a couple of losers. You deserve each other," and with that the old man set off down the road in search of a new horse to replace the lame counterpart.

Adam now realised that by struggling in defending the horse he was in fact making himself sink more; the more he struggled, the deeper he sank. So, for the next ten minutes or so, in the relative calm without the presence of the old man, he leaned over and stroked the exhausted grey horse. The tired, terrified animal gradually began to calm under the calming influence of the small boy.

When the horse had finally regained its breath and composure, it was able to stand and free itself from the thick mud that had temporarily imprisoned it. Now it was Adam's turn to escape. However, this turned out to be easier than expected as the horse leant over swaying its reins over towards the struggling child. He thankfully grabbed the reins and smiled as the horse swiftly lifted him clean of the mud.

Back on solid ground, Adam stroked his new friend on the nose. Looking down, he noticed a deep cut in the horse's leg, blood gushing out, despite the mud and a large wooden splint sticking out, the cause of the lameness. Still stroking and reassuring his new friend, he carefully removed the splint from his leg and, taking off his cloak, made a temporary bandage around the horse's leg to prevent further bleeding.

"I think I'll call you Smokie," Adam decided.

If Smokie could say thanks, it would have but a friendly nuzzle with its new master was equally appreciated by the page. The pair spent a few minutes, offering comfort to each other, until rudely interrupted by a procession of horses and carriages thundering down the track they stood at the side of.

Chapter 3

The train of horses and the elaborate carriages they pulled stopped by the page and his new friend. As the huge dust cloud they had created settled, Adam could see a luxurious carriage stood in front of him, covered in ornate design and thick, red, plush drapes over the windows.

Unsure of the passenger of such a sophisticated mode of transport Adam stroked his new friend on the nose and kept him close, like a security blanket. Finally, the curtain over the window moved and the face of a bearded man smiled kindly at him.

"You boy, come here," he called. "Is this the road to the home of Sir Wilf of Whiffington?"

"Yes, my lord," for that is whom the page believed he was talking to, "it is." Adam now looked at the crest upon the carriage door and the flags that fluttered limply in the lack of breeze. He saw the colours red and black but did not recognise the crest which included a tiger.

"I am Sir Victor of Astley and I am the new Lord of Sir Wilf's land. Are you familiar with this gentleman?"

"I am indeed," came the reply. "He was my former master."

"Then where are you heading if your home is back there?"

"I want to become a knight and I am heading to Knight School. There is nothing left for me back home. It is time for me to move onto the next stage of my life."

"Knight School, eh?" answered the powerful looking lord. "I think you might be better off if you turn around and head home."

"Why would I do that?"

"Because I am always in need of another page and if you are good at what you do, I will put you forward for Knight School myself. How does that sound?"

Adam thought to himself. The day had not quite gone as he had planned: he had hoped to be much further on his journey than he was but the ordeal with the horse had held him up. Now he had the opportunity to work under a new master; one who had said they would put him through to Knight School if he works hard.

"That is very kind of you my lord," answered Adam. Perhaps the day would end more positively after all.

"That is very pleasing to me," Sir Victor replied. "Now get yourself back home. What is your name?"

"Adam," came the reply and with that the knight sat back in his seat and pounded on the ceiling of his carriage as a sign for the driver to set off. With another cloud of dust, the Lord disappeared into the distance leaving Adam alone with his horse, or so he thought.

As the dust settled, Adam found himself surrounded by a group of boys similar in age to him. From the clothing they were wearing, he could tell that they too were pages, something that they would make very clear very quickly.

"Who do you think you are?" threatened one boy.

"You don't belong in our group. Best if you clear off," followed another.

"Look at that horse. It's nearly as pathetic as you," retorted a third.

The cruel comments continued but Adam noticed all the boys suddenly became quiet when one tall, skinny, blonde haired boy moved to the front of the group.

"Look at what we have here lads. Another page. Hoping to take one of your roles no doubt. Well we can't be having that then, can we?"

"No Atticus," chorused the other pages.

"So what shall we do with you?" the leader now addressed Adam for the first time. "My name is Atticus and I am Sir Victor's favourite and best page. I think it would be advisable for you if you don't return as the master said and continue on your way."

"Sir Victor asked me to go back to help him and that is what I will do," replied Adam.

"Is that right?" Atticus responded. "Now you listen to me. I am the best page; I do all the favoured jobs and I will certainly be the one who Sir Victor picks to go to Knight School. I am the strongest. I am the tallest. I am the cleverest. I am the greatest. Anyone got a problem with that and they will find out the hard way that they should never cross me. Do you want to cross me?"

"I don't want anything to do with you." Adam replied. "I just want to get out of this mud and get back home."

"Ha," Atticus laughed. "You my friend are going nowhere. In fact, you and your lame friend here can stay in that mud until you starve."

With that, Atticus pushed Adam back towards the mud. Adam did not like to be pushed and he was always taught to stand up for himself.

"Don't push me," Adam grimaced through clenched teeth.

"I will do whatever I like and there is nothing you can do about it," Atticus replied. Adam moved forward towards Atticus and pushed the tall boy away from him.

Atticus did not like this one bit. He was used to being in charge, having others cower at his mere presence, not being pushed around by some stranger who he had no respect for at all.

"Right, that does it," warned Atticus and as he stood, he produced his sword and pointed it in the direction of Adam. "Time for me to teach you a lesson."

Adam was unsure what to do. As pages they should not be fighting each other, but in this very second, he felt like he had no choice other than to defend himself.

He reached to his side and pulled out his trust wooden blade.

"Ha ha ha. Is that it?" Atticus fell about laughing at Adam's primitive weapon.

"It may not be metal or as fancy as yours, but I am not afraid to use it."

"Ok then," Atticus responded. " Let's see what you are made of."

The two boys began to duel and, although at a serious disadvantage, Adam held his own. Or he did until Atticus took a quick swipe and sliced straight through the end of Adam's wooden blade.

The watching boys laughed and jeered at Adam, but Adam's spirit was true and he continued the battle. Again, he fought gallantly until another blow and more of his wooden blade was snapped off.

The boys now were gathering around Adam, pushing him further back towards the mud. Realising he was in a tight spot, Adam tried to push his way past the boys but with no luck. He threw what remained of his wooden sword at the pages but nothing. Eventually, they were all on top of him and grabbed him one limb each and carried him to the mud.

Adam was unceremoniously dumped in the mud and as he sank to new depths, he could see the boys laughing and joking as they rode off towards his home leaving his sword in several pieces all over the floor.

Chapter 4

Whiffington Hall was no more. Not only was it a ridiculous name for a grand old house, but now Sir Wilf had died (on the toilet) with no heir, it was up to the new Lord to decide the name.

The Whiffington's had lived there for over a hundred years. Many things had changed in that time, and on the whole, they were for the worse.

Sir Wilf had taken everything from the people who lived on his lands, charging them excessive amounts of money to live under his protection. If the people did not have money, they paid using what they could. This could include grain, vegetables, cattle, weapons or even offering themselves as his servants. Sir Wilf just took, took, took. He did not give anything back to the people. Because of this, many left but soon, people were so poor they could not afford to leave so they had to stay in his service.

Sir Wilf's ancestors had not been as cruel, looking after the community and making the whole area thrive. Sir Wilf had been a spoilt brat since he was born. As a teenager, he used to make fun of the poor and treat them terribly, so when the day came for him to be in charge of the land, many of the townsfolk left in search of a better life.

Adam had never known any different. He had always been a servant of some sort. He thought that was normal for a boy of his age. Now, the presence of Sir Victor made him hopeful of change, though he still wasn't sure of the other pages.

They had all been summoned to the courtyard by Sir Victor. He had begun to settle into his new home but found many things needed attending to or repairing. (Sir Wilf had also let the place go to ruin).

"Now that you are all here..." he started. "Hang on a moment, where is Adam, the young boy I met on the road?" Atticus cleared his throat to lie.

"He carried on his way. To Knight School I assume," the boy sniggered, joined by his gang of thugs behind him.

"Well that is very strange as I asked him to come back to be a page. Are you certain of this Atticus?" Before he could answer, there was a commotion by the gate and as the crowd parted, Sir Victor and the pages could see Adam stumbling across the courtyard with his new friend, Smokie, loyally behind. The pages continued their laughing and began pointing at the couple, much to their amusement. However, this was not to Sir Victor's amusement.

"You boys, be quiet!" he commanded. The laughs drained away to tiny sniggers and soon silence was restored. "Good to see you again Adam."

"Not likely," one of the pages called out from the back of the group. Adam had had enough. He had spent the whole day walking or falling in mud and he was not in the mood for more humiliation from the new pages.

He stepped forward towards the gang of boys, and as he let go of the reins of his horse, he pulled out his sword, forgetting what had happened earlier. Standing there, with less than half of a broken, wooden sword, he felt angry, but managed to control his temper in front of his new master.

"Now tell me Adam, what has happened to you?" Adam's initial thought was to tell the truth, but the feeling of honour among pages made him explain a little differently.

"I fell off my horse on the way back and then got stuck in some mud. I have been walking back all day as my new horse has an injured leg.

"And how did your sword break?" asked Sir Victor, not convinced by the boy's words.

"Err, I had a fight with a man about this horse," lied Adam. "He was mistreating it and I had to do something to protect it."

"That is very noble of you," praised Sir Victor. "Now let's have a look at that sword."

"It's broken my Lord," responded Adam. "I think I am going to have to get a new one."

"I think I may be able to help," replied the Lord. "Atticus, fetch my personal chest." Adam could hear the page mumbling to himself as he and two other pages disappeared round the back of the carriage. A couple of minutes later, they appeared again, huffing and puffing as they lifted a huge chest towards their master.

"Thank you," said Sir Victor. They dropped the chest to the floor with a loud thud and Sir Victor carefully opened the wooden box. He rummaged around inside for a couple of minutes and eventually emerged with a very old, but magnificent looking sword.

In his hands, this sword looked tiny but he strode over to Adam and presented it to him.

"When I was your age, I went to Knight School and this was my trusty sword. It may be old and look a little worn, but I think it is in good hands if I pass it on to you."

Adam could not believe his ears. A real sword. Okay, it was old and a little rusty but it was a real sword, given by his new master.

"Take care of that Adam," insisted Sir Victor. "It has been in my family for a long time. I expect you to use it honourably and only in times of need. You have much to learn as a young page. You all do."

He now turned to all the other pages who were mumbling amongst themselves.

"Take a lesson from young Adam here. He left his home to seek out a better life for himself and because of this he is now set on a new path. You pages can learn a lesson here. Follow your dreams and you will be rewarded."

Atticus was not one bit happy. He could not believe Sir Victor had given the sword to Adam. It should have been his, he thought to himself. He was the lead page. This was a big moment, as a Lord, if he had no children of his own, he would pass on his first sword to his favourite page. Here he was, his master, Sir Victor, giving it to a new page he did not even know. This incensed Atticus beyond belief and only made his hatred for Adam even more.

"You just wait," Atticus mumbled under his breath. "My day will come, and when it does, that page had better watch out!"

Chapter 5

And so the journey of being a page to a new master began for Adam. The actual training of being a page was hard work but Adam enjoyed every second of it. The taunting and mocking from the other pages, however, was not enjoyable.

No matter what he did, Adam suffered continual ridicule from his peers, especially Atticus, but he tried his best to carry on regardless. So what does a typical day for a page look like?

First job of the day is to be up before everyone else. Why? Because they had to light the fires. Imagine tiptoeing around a huge, freezing cold house, terrified you may wake someone up, especially the master. Everything is pitch black as all the previous night's fires lie smouldering in empty hearths.

A long journey to the kitchen to the one fire that remained lit all night. If you were the unlucky page at that time, you had to stay awake all night to ensure the fire did not go out. Once someone had come to relieve you, you could then get a few hours sleep.

The fire lighter would then take a tapered candle and carefully move around the main rooms of the house preparing to light a fire. However, the fire needed to be built first. To start, a small pile of kindling was built and fresh straw added.

This was lit and encouraged and as the fire got bigger, larger logs were added to make the fire grow. Success, but it had to be repeated several times throughout the house. The only advantage was the heat generated enabled the fire lighting page to eventually warm up.

However, shifting many large logs also warmed up the page in question so before they knew it, they had gone from freezing cold to boiling hot.

Now that the fires were lit, the master's room needed to be prepared. Again, a tricky job as not only did you have a long list of tasks, but you also had to do them in the dark and silence.

The first job was to crawl around the floor and find any clothing, armour or weapons that may have been left on the floor. These then needed to be left tidy in the appropriate place ready for the next day.

If the master kept his dog or dogs in the bedroom, then their water and food needed changing. It was not easy keeping quiet when bringing food in for a dog!

Next, the worst job. Emptying the chamber pot. This could go one of two ways – an easy job as it was empty, or a horrific job as it full. You could tell from the smell whether it was going to be a good or bad job!

All of this had to be done by seven o'clock in the morning as that is what time the new master awoke. (It was much better when Sir Wilf was master as he used to stay in bed till eleven every day).

Once the master awoke, another servant would bring food if required in bed. Sir Wilf always ate breakfast in bed. Come to mention it, Sir Wilf ate most meals in bed.

Sir Victor on the other hand, was up early at seven. He wanted to go on an early morning ride every day so breakfast would have to wait.

The page would have to prepare the clothing Sir Victor would wear for his morning ride. This did not just mean laying the clothes out, they also needed to be washed from the previous day.

Again, Sir Wilf rarely changed his clothes, but Sir Victor had higher hygiene standards so his clothes had to be washed and dried overnight, another task for a page.

When the master was ready to leave for his morning ride, the page would have to accompany and be at the beck and call of the Lord.

If the master was hunting with a crossbow, the page may have to prepare the weapon, ensure it is clean and reload after an arrow has been found. If the master is successful in the hunt, the page would have to collect whatever the game the master had targeted.

When returning home, Sir Victor would then eat his breakfast which a page would have to serve.

Following this, the page may have some time to themselves but this would not last for long. They may have to pass messages on for Sir Victor. This may be to someone else in the house or it could be miles way, requiring a journey by horse.

Weapons had to be cleaned and cared for daily. A visit to the blacksmith with a sword or dagger for resharpening, cleaning arrows or shields and checking chain mail for any holes or weaknesses.

Continuing on from weapons would be combat training. Here the master would work with the pages to teach them the basics of combat. This involved practise, practise and more practise. This included swordsmanship, defence, target practise with a crossbow and catapult, jousting and all of these again but on horseback.

Though his days were hard, Adam saw his days as a form of education not labour. He received no payment for his chores but he did get clothing, accommodation and food. Adam actually enjoyed the whole experience and worked hard. He wanted to be the number one page and, in turn, go to Knight School. Atticus however, felt that this position was his.

Atticus was a very influential boy and had many of the other pages doing his tasks for him. How had he got to this level? Through bullying and intimidation.

Adam had witnessed this at first hand but he did not like it. He kept away from Atticus as much as possible. He did not want to be involved in his underhand dealings. He witnessed Atticus beating smaller, younger pages if they refused to do his tasks. He saw Atticus taking food meant for the master and eating it himself, but then blaming others for the loss and laughing when they were punished.

Adam thought to himself if he just stayed out of the way, kept his head down and carried on with his chores he would be rewarded in the end. However, this was easier said than done as Atticus had made it his priority to pick on those he felt were a threat to him and, as the weeks and months went by, with Sir Victor as the new Lord, Adam was rapidly becoming the centre of attention.

Chapter 6

There had been many confrontations between Adam and Atticus in the short period of time they had been together. Atticus would mock Adam calling him Sir Victor's pet and favourite (something which Adam though Atticus was only jealous of).

Sir Victor had really taken to Adam. He could see the hard work the young boy put in and he was often rewarded for his work with special treats.

These included further training, days off (which Adam never took) or special one-off events. Today was such a day. Adam was to learn about falconry. There was to be a gathering at a castle several miles away, the home of another Lord, and Sir Victor was invited. This would involve two days travel and a night staying over.

Sir Victor had made it known that he needed a page to go with him. Atticus felt he was the page for the job and almost expected to be picked. It seemed to Adam that this was the most likely outcome, so he gave it no further thought.

On the day of announcement, Adam was continuing his chores. Today he was taking the scraps out of the kitchen to the pigs that lived just outside the main gates.

Adam enjoyed this, despite the smell, as it got him out in the fresh air and he felt pigs were such funny creatures with their funny snouts, strange noises and curly tails. As he approached the sty, he noticed a small boy in the pen rooting through the trough, obviously looking for food.

"What are you doing there?" Adam asked the boy. There was no response, just the look of fear upon the small child's face.

"Are you eating the pig's food?" The boy solemnly nodded. "Where are you from?"

"I don't really know," answered the boy. "I have been walking for miles and found this place. I sleep with the pigs at night as they keep me warm and I have been sharing their food."

"Well you can't do that!" Adam responded.

"I'm sorry, please do not turn me in," begged the boy.

"I'm not going to do that. I will get you some proper food. Stay there. I promise no harm will come to you." And with that, Adam set off for the main house and entered the kitchen. Here, he saw the room that never sleeps. People were always preparing food, serving, then tidying up. This was a cycle that continued all day (and often night) every single day.

The main cook, Benedict, could always be found chopping meat, or stirring the huge cauldron above the fire. He liked his meat cleaver and always had it to hand. Adam often wondered if he would use it for other things than cooking. Adam was about to take some food from the kitchen for the small boy he met and did not want to find out if Benedict used the cleaver to punish thieves.

He had managed to remain in the shadows at the back of the room, waiting for his moment to arise. Having already picked up an apple and carrot from the vegetable rack in the store, Adam was now after some bread.

Fresh bread was kept near the fire as Benedict loved the smell when it had just been baked. Stealthily, Adam approached the fire and, whilst hiding under a large table, managed to grab a chunk of bread and return his hand under the table (thankfully still attached to his arm).

Hiding his stolen possessions as much as he could, Adam left the kitchen and returned to the sty. The boy was nowhere to be seen. Adam searched for him and eventually found the boy behind the sty, drinking water from a dirty puddle.

"Another boy came so I had to hide," mumbled the child.

"Look what I have got you," Adam responded. He emptied his pockets and gave the boy his trove.

"Is that for me?"

"Well of course it is," Adam replied. "And I will try and get you some more whilst you are here."

"That is so kind of you," the boy whispered, almost close to tears.

"Don't you worry, I have been in your position and know how it feels," Adam reassured.

"Know how what feels?" came a voice from behind. Adam spun round and saw Atticus. "What's going on here?"

"Nothing. Get lost Atticus," Adam replied.

"Now, now. Don't be like that. Who have we got here?" Atticus had now shifted his attention to the small boy who was cowering behind Adam.

"Nothing for you to see here," Adam answered. Atticus noticed the food the boy was shovelling into his mouth.

"Where did you get that? From the kitchen? Have you been stealing from the master? Wait till I tell him what has been going on here."

"This is nothing to do with you. Go away," Adam repeated.

"Or what?" taunted Atticus. Adam tried to ignore the situation but could see he was in a tricky position. "I'm going to tell the master."

Adam ran across the pig sty and flung the gate open, grabbing onto the back of Atticus. With all his might he swung round and threw Atticus towards the pig sty. As he did, the spring-loaded gate was closing, hitting Atticus in his mid-drift and sending him flying, head over heels into the pen.

The small boy began to laugh but Atticus was not in a laughing mood. He rose to his feet and headed out of the sty back towards the main house.

"Are you ok?" Adam asked the small boy. The boy nodded. "I suggest you find somewhere to hide and I will come and find you tomorrow." Again the boy nodded and Adam turned and headed back to the house unsure of what would happen next.

Atticus had already made it to Sir Victor and was taking great delight in telling him what had happened.

"Is this true Adam? Have you stolen food from the kitchen to feed a runaway boy?" Adam nodded and accepted that he needed to be punished for his behaviour. He did not expect what happened next.

"Who can tell me the virtues of being a knight?" questioned Sir Victor.

"Courage and justice," shouted Atticus whilst grinning at Adam.

"What else?" Sir Victor continued. Various answers came from the surrounding pages.

"Mercy."

"Generosity."

"Faith."

"Nobility."

"Hope."

"Excellent," Sir Victor continued. "You are all excellent students. However, learning these virtues is one thing, but they count for nothing if they are not followed. Adam, why did you steal the food?"

"Because the child was hungry and had nothing."

"That sounds like mercy and generosity to me," Sir Victor commented. "And I'm sure it took courage to steal from my kitchen." Adam nodded solemnly. "Which leads me on to justice."

"He needs to pay for what he has done," Atticus blurted out.

"I think I know what needs to be done, thank you very much Atticus." Atticus now became silent. He felt sure Adam was going to receive the punishment he deserved for this crime.

"So justice needs to be served. Do you accept your punishment, Adam?"

"I do Sir Victor," replied Adam.

"Very well, you will attend the falconry event with me and will be the lead page for the days we are away."

"But... Sir… I don't understand."

"As far as I can see, you have shown three virtues of a knight and were happy to receive justice for what you did, so that makes four."

Atticus could not believe what he was hearing.

"My Lord I must protest."

"No Atticus," replied Sir Victor, "I protest. You could learn a lot from this and I insist you change your clothes. You smell like a pig sty."

Chapter 7

Showing the virtues of a knight had earnt Adam his role as primary page to Sir Victor at the falconry event. Here, he learnt many skills including how to train a hawk to hunt for rabbit or squirrel. Essential skills for any knight and he was very grateful.

However, it was the time he spent with Sir Victor that meant most. He not only taught him vital skills for a knight, but also how to think and behave. The value of the virtues.

Adam had never known his father and saw Sir Victor as a father figure. He was a great role model for him, so much better that Sir

Wilf was. Adam listened to everything he said and acted upon it. This impressed Sir Victor immensely but Atticus did not like it one bit.

Atticus felt it was time to regain his position as top page so decided on a cunning plan to put him back where he thought he belonged.

Sir Victor had left for a week and had decided to go alone. He explained there was an evil presence in the land. He needed to meet with other knights in a secret location to discuss the unsavoury actions that had been happening across the area.

"I wonder what it is?" asked Adam.

"I don't know but it sounds quite serious, especially if Sir Victor is going alone to this meeting," Eleanor answered.

"I'm sure he must need some help," Adam thought.

"Keep out of it you, just because you're the favourite," Atticus butted in.

"Get lost Atticus, this is nothing to do with you." Adam had little time for Atticus now and mocking from his rival was not something he was interested in.

As Sir Victor was away for a week, the pages had much more time to themselves. Adam and Eleanor spent most of the time together, Eleanor helping Adam with his training when they weren't doing chores.

On the day of Sir Victor's return, they decided to visit the jousting arena. This place was desolate at the moment but when jousting tournaments took place it was the most magnificent place to be. Visiting Lords and Knights would battle against each other and pages would prepare them for their joust. It was the highlight of the year for a page as it was a chance to show off their skills, meet friends from other lands and hope their master wins.

Jousting involved two horse riders holding lances (long, blunt, wooden poles) racing towards each other as was done in battle. The aim of the joust was to try and strike the opponent, breaking the lance on the shield or armour or, if possible, dismounting the opponent.

Eleanor and Adam stood on the jousting field both reminiscing of past jousts and imagining future ones.

"Just imagine what it must be like, riding down here towards another knight with a lance only to protect you," Eleanor sighed.

"I know, I hope I get to do it one day," Adam answered.

"I'm sure you will," Eleanor replied. "You are by far the best page and will surely be picked for Knight School. I'm so jealous of you and wish I could be a page"

"You'd be a great page," Adam beamed. "Better than me. It's not fair that you can't be one. Imagine if we could go to Knight School together."

"Neither of you will be going," came a voice from behind. "That place is mine."

"Go away Atticus, you're not welcome here," Eleanor shouted.

"Ooooo!" replied Atticus and his cronies. "This is no place for a girl," Atticus continued.

"Don't you say things like that. Eleanor is far better than you," Adam jumped in.

"Ha, she is just a girl," Atticus continued knowing it would provoke Adam.

"I'll show you," Eleanor argued. "What is your choice of battle?"

"Ha ha, as if you could do that," Atticus mocked.

"Pick then," demanded Eleanor, determined to silence this annoyance.

"Joust," answered Atticus, "let's see you do that. I bet you can't even carry a lance."

"Okay, joust it is."

"Are you mad?" Adam interjected. "You can't do this."

"Oh so you think I can't do this either?" moaned Eleanor.

"Not at all, but you will get into trouble," reasoned Adam.

"Well what choice do I have now?" answered Eleanor, beginning to regret her decision now.

"Leave it to me," Adam reassured. "Atticus, this is against the page's rules. You cannot do this."

"Oh, so you are both chicken then," and with that he pushed Adam over. Eleanor lost her temper and went for Atticus. All of his friends were laughing and mocking her but soon stopped when she threw a punch in Atticus' direction and knocked him to the floor.

Atticus was so shocked and almost lost for words. His cronies did not know whether to laugh or fight back. As it turned out they did neither and just stood there gobsmacked with blank faces.

"You... you... can't... do ... that!" mumbled Atticus. He appeared to be suffering from a mild concussion and was struggling to string words together in a sentence.

Suddenly, a trumpet fanfare could be heard in this distance. This could mean only one thing; Sir Victor was almost home.

"I think you better leave Eleanor," Adam decided. "I'll sort this out."

"Oh no, what have I done," Eleanor panicked.

"I'll sort it. You get back to the house."

The sound of the horn had an effect on the surrounding gang of pages. They all shuffled off towards the house, leaving Adam and Atticus alone.

"Are you ok?" Adam asked through gritted teeth.

"I'm not sure what has happened. I… feel… a… bit…" and then nothing. Atticus passed out and slumped to the floor.

"Great!" Adam sighed. As he stood over the collapsed page, he felt the rumble of horses through the floor, and sure enough, Sir Victor appeared.

"What is going on here?" Sir Victor quizzed. Adam jumped straight in with a lie.

"Atticus and I had a fight. He deserved it but unfortunately, he appears to have been knocked out."

"Fighting among pages? You know this is not part of the code. This is not appropriate behaviour. I will see you in my study back at the house. I suggest you get this excuse for a page back to the house."

"How do I do that?" Adam asked.

"Not my problem," Sir Victor boomed. He was not happy.

"This is not the sort of behaviour I would expect from a potential for Knight School."

Chapter 8

Adam felt terrible. He was glad he had saved Eleanor from getting into trouble and that Atticus was still unconscious on the floor, but now he had to suffer the wrath of Sir Victor.

After putting Atticus on Smokie's back and finally getting back to the house, Adam walked the long, daunting corridor to Sir Victor's study. As he approached the door, Adam gulped and slowly knocked on the door.

"Enter," boomed a voice from inside. Adam pushed the heavy, oak door and entered.

Sir Victor's study was the room in which he spent most time. He had a large open fire that was roaring as Adam moved across the room to the enormous desk, against which Sir Victor was leaning.

Although this was not his bedroom, there was a bed in the corner of the room, from the days of Sir Wilf who basically lived in bed. Two gigantic hounds named Ollie and Layla lay in front of the fire, lifting their heads to see if a threat was approaching but returning back to their slumber.

The wall was adorned by various shields, swords and hunting prizes. Adam knew all the swords were from important battles Sir Victor had taken part in as a knight. A stag's head was the largest of the appendages trying to escape the wall.

"Well," Sir Victor began. "What do you have to say for yourself?"

"I am sorry I have let you down but…" Adam paused.

"But what?"

"Is Atticus okay?"

"Yes, he is," Sir Victor reassured.

"Atticus deserved it," Adam continued. "He was being unfair to Eleanor. She is my friend and I will not let anything happen to her."

"Very noble Adam, but there has to be some punishment." As Sir Victor finished his sentence the door to his study suddenly flung open and in ran Eleanor.

"It wasn't Adam. It was me. I hit Atticus because he was not being very nice to me. Please don't punish Adam for something he hasn't done."

"This is most unusual," Sir Victor answered. "Is this true Adam?"

"No it was me," Adam lied again.

"So I now have two people taking blame for attacking a page. I suppose I shall just have to ask Atticus" Adam knew he was for it now. He would now be in trouble for lying to his master and the punishment for that would be banishment. He would be told to leave.

"As it happens, I have already had this discussion with Atticus. The fool has told me exactly what happened. So this is what is going to happen."

The pair stood next to each other, both expecting the worst possible news.

"Eleanor, you have shown incredible bravery in standing up to a bully. This courage will not go unnoticed. I am therefore in need of a new page and the job is your if you wish."

"I don't know what to say," Eleanor gasped.

"Say yes," Sir Victor prompted.

"Yes," beamed Eleanor. It is what she had dreamt of and could not quite believe this moment was happening.

"As for you young man," Sir Victor continued, "I am not happy that you lied to me but again you have shown courage and nobility in protecting Eleanor and for that you must be commended. Now I suggest you two get out of my sight before I change my mind. Soon, I will decide who will be going to Knight School.

That day soon came around and all the pages were summoned into the courtyard, surrounded by many of the townsfolk, eager to see who would be picked.

Bunting had been put up around the square and everyone was in a happy mood. This event was a highlight of the year and everyone celebrated it.

Later on in the day, there would be a party were the winning page would wear a wooden crown and everyone would make a huge fuss of them. Although girls had not been included before, today was extra special for Eleanor, the first female page up for a position at Knight School.

Sir Victor was welcomed into the courtyard with warm applause and gave a speech. In this speech, he even mentioned how hard

Eleanor had worked in her page training and that she had shown true bravery in tough situations.

Sir Victor had a scroll in his hand and, after his speech, was about to unroll it, but a trumpet fanfare broke through the excitement, changing the atmosphere to one of panic. Something was happening. What could it be? The fanfare was used to signal the arrival of the master, but if the master was at home, it meant important news was coming.

Sir Victor replaced the scroll into his pocket and announced that the ceremony would have to wait. The gates swung open and a rider entered the arena.

"Sir Victor, it is just as we feared. He is coming."

Chapter 9

Adam was unsure who they were referring to but he knew it sounded serious. Sir Victor looked anxious and made an announcement.

"We are entering a difficult situation and we need to take some protection. I need to leave and will take three pages with me. When I have gone, you will need to ensure all the villagers are in the town walls, raise the drawbridge and have a continual guard present on the walls."

There were nervous murmurs among the crowd but Sir Victor continued.

"The Black Knight and his followers have been spotted terrorising nearby villages. This is not a situation I am happy with so I must act. A couple of knights and I have been meeting regularly, keeping up to date with events and now is the time to move. I require Atticus, Eleanor and Adam. Get your things together; we leave in one hour."

Eleanor and Adam ran to their rooms and got together the things they needed. As pages, they would not need much equipment for themselves, but they had to make sure they had everything Sir Victor needed. They had a list for such occasions and it included many different items:

- Armour – this is the plate armour (the heavy stuff) which offers the most protection. All the pieces had special names, for example – gauntlets for hands, greaves for ankles and calves, pauldron for shoulders and, of course, helmet for head. A page's job was to help dress the knight and ensure it was clean and shiny.

- Chain mail – this was made from thousands of metal rings. Because of this it was flexible and offered good protection. A page had to make sure there were no gaps in the chain mail.

- Lance – the long wooden pole with a metal tip and hand guards. This provided a huge advantage against foot soldiers and against other knights on horseback. The page would have to make sure it was not splintered or ready to break.

- Sword – the preferred weapon. Some were one handed while others chose the larger two-handed sword. The page must ensure it was sharpened.

- Mace – a club with a big steel head

- Longbow – excellent for attacking from a distance

- Horse – trained for battle and Sir Victor's was called Destrier. It also required armour, sorted by the page.

There were many other accessories required. Part of a page's training was practising dressing the master in their armour.

The time to leave had arrived and the pages had done their tasks dutifully. Sir Victor mounted his battle horse and led the procession including the carriage with the pages and all the supplies.

As they crossed the drawbridge and trundled down the road, Adam saw the drawbridge being raised. They were on their way to battle.

"We are heading over to the next town, Chorley. That is where the Black Knight was last seen," announced Sir Victor.

The journey took over half an hour but it was easy to see where they were heading as huge plumes of smoke rose into the sky. The town of Chorley was on fire.

The Black Knight and his men attacked villages, took what they wanted and then destroyed what was left. They then moved from village to town with no one to stop them. This is why Sir Victor had arranged with a group of other knights to do something about it before any more people lost their lives or towns were destroyed.

As they pulled up on the outskirts of the town, Sir Victor ordered the convoy to stop and make camp. This was the meeting point for all the knights and an excellent vantage point where the knights could attack from.

Tents were thrown up quickly and the knights discussed their plan. And as quickly as that, they were dressed, mounted their horses and set off for battle.

The pages now had to sit around and wait. Some may be used as messengers but on the whole, they had to wait for their master to return, whether it be in victory, in need of reinforcement or defeat.

Close to the tents was a small wood of high trees. Adam told Eleanor he was going for a better view of the battle. The pair set off and climbed the tallest tree they could.

From their new vantage point they could see the whole of the town and the battle that was taking place outside the town walls.

"Things don't look good," Eleanor said in despair.

"I know, the Black Knight seems to have far more knights than first thought." From their spot, they could see the black flags of the evil presence in the land and there were plenty.

"This isn't going to be a fair fight. They are walking into a trap," Adam continued.

"What can we do?" Eleanor added.

"We will stay here out of harm," came a familiar voice. It was Atticus. With paying so much attention to the battle, they had not seen him climb their tree.

"We need to do something," Adam shouted angrily. "Staying here is not helping."

"Look!" exclaimed Eleanor as she pointed at a group of horse moving away from the battle. "Those knights are leaving the battle."

"And look where they are heading, HOME!" added Adam. "We must go back and help them."

"Are you mad?" Atticus interjected. "We were told to say here. Those were our orders."

"Well you stay here and follow orders. We have friends and family who need our help."

Adam shot down the tree and headed to the cart. Eleanor followed closely, concerned about her mother back at the house.

"What's the plan?" she quizzed.

"I don't know, I'm making this up as I go along," Adam answered honestly. With that, they climbed on Smokie and set off for home. The journey was much quicker on horseback at full speed than it had been earlier. As they turned up back at home, a terrifying sight awaited them.

A group of knights were attacking the walls with longbows and a battering ram was being used on the drawbridge.

"Woah Smokie," Adam called. The pair jumped off the horse and hid behind a mound just outside of town.

"Now what?" Adam asked.

"Let's save our town," Eleanor beamed proudly.

"And how can we do that?" Adam added.

Eleanor set off towards the knights. Adam followed, unsure what she may have planned, but they had to do something.

"All we need to do is cause a distraction. Stop them from attacking the house."

"Yes," Adam added. "Sir Victor will be back soon. I hope."

Chapter 10

The attacking knights had taken a break from attacking the home of the pages and were now lined up on their horses, planning their next move.

Adam had an idea. He told Eleanor to stay where she was until he gave her a signal. Then, she was to make a distraction of some sort. Adam crawled round the edge of the field the knights were gathered and like a snake he slid directly behind the horses.

Now this was not an ideal place to be at the best of times. The rear of a horse was bad for many reasons. Adam's plan was simple;

crawl under the horses and undo the strapping for the saddle. Then, Eleanor causes a distraction and all the knights are dismounted.

The plan went perfectly apart from one horse that Adam could not sort. One knight on horseback would be much better than all of them so Adam continued with the plan.

He could see Eleanor in the distance and as he crawled back to a safe distance, he made his signal.

"Help, help," screamed Eleanor, running from the mound she was hid behind.

"Get her," came a deep, booming voice and the knights set off. It was quite a sight to see, several knights setting off at full gallop then rapidly realising their saddle was no longer attached to the horse beneath. A couple fell from their horses, landing uncomfortably on the ground. The others, realising their problem, dropped their lances and clung on for dear life as their transport headed off in varying directions.

What Adam had not taken into consideration was the remaining knight on horseback and what was even worse was the realisation that this knight was, in fact, the Black Knight. Amidst all the confusion this Knight remained calm and turn his horse around facing Adam. Now he was in trouble.

"You boy," he boomed, "I will take great pleasure in defeating you."

He leapt from his horse and landed on the ground with a thud. He drew his immense two-handed sword and swung it round his head. Adam stood, terrified but courage was on his side. He withdrew his sword, no comparison to the Black Knight's, but he stood and faced his foe.

"This will be easy," the Black Knight exclaimed as he swung his sword towards Adam. Swinging his tiny sword in an attempt to defend himself, Adam realised he was done for. Or was he?

As the Black Knight swung his sword to crush his victim an arrow shot through the air and embedded itself in the chink between the gauntlet on the hand and the plate covering the forearm. It was a million to one shot but luckily for Adam, it was one that made the Black Knight drop his sword.

Where had it come from? And then he realised. There stood Eleanor with a cross bow in her hands. She had saved him. The Black Knight was not finished though, as he snapped the arrow in two freeing his wrist. Sustaining a terrible injury, this knight still continued and, one handed, reached for his sword again.

He swung and swung the sword with all his might, but only using his weaker hand, it was useless. Suddenly, there was fanfare of trumpets. Coming over the hill in the distance, Adam could see the flags and colours of Sir Victor.

Realising he was fighting a losing battle against a page; he knew he stood no chance against Sir Victor and his knights. He moved to his horse and awkwardly mounted it. He set off, riding in the complete opposite way to Sir Victor.

"What do you think you are doing?" Sir Victor called to Adam.

"I...I...I... was trying to help," stammered Adam.

"It is not your position to decide, you were given orders and you have not followed them." Sir Victor looked disappointed.

"I'm sorry," answered Adam. He felt so disappointed.

"If it weren't for Atticus doing his job and passing on messages, you would be gone now. Do you understand?"

Adam listened to the words and his heart sank. He realised he had let everyone down. He looked up to find Eleanor but could see her nowhere. All he saw was the smug grin of Atticus.

All had returned to normal. The towns had been restored and life was as it was. The day had come. Sir Victor was to announce who was in line for Knight School. Adam already knew the result but came along to the ceremony to show his support as a page.

"Well done Atticus," announced Sir Victor. "You have shown great skill and loyalty to your master and I reward this with a place at Knight School." Applause followed and Atticus waved egotistically to the crowd.

"But there is more…" Sir Victor continued. "This person has shown such improvement and it is my decision that Eleanor will also attend Knight School."

This made Adam smile. His best friend was being rewarded for all the hard work she had done. He grinned at his friend and she returned the expression.

The ceremony finished and as the people left the courtyard, Sir Victor made his way to Adam.

"Since I have been here, you have shown courage, justice, mercy, generosity, faith, nobility and hope. All the virtues of a knight. However, you have also shown recklessness and disobedience. These are not the virtues of a knight, but they are those of a boy who looks after his friends, tries to do good and puts others first. So Adam... you are also going to Knight School, but you must work on these things. I will be in close contact to check your progression but you will leave with the others."

Adam could not believe this. His dream had come true and what's more, he was going with his best friend. He did not know what the future would hold but he did know it involved him going to Knight School.

Other titles by Chris Allton include:

Please visit
www.chrisallton.co.uk
for more information.

Printed in Great Britain
by Amazon